RONNIE'S WISH

by

JEANETTE
PERKINS BROWN

drawings by
JEAN MARTINEZ

RONNIE'S WISH

by
Jeanette Perkins Brown

DRAWINGS BY
Jean Martinez

FRIENDSHIP PRESS • NEW YORK

SECOND PRINTING JANUARY 1959

Format by Louise E. Jefferson
Library of Congress Catalog Card Number 54-6957

Ronnie wished he weren't so little. His eyes came just to
the counter at the grocery store in his block.

When his mother sent him on an errand, there were always
grown-up people ahead of him, and the grocery man noticed
them first.

3

There were the tall ladies who made the grocery man look
up at them instead of down at him.

There were the large ladies who crowded him quite out
of sight of the grocery man.

There were the big, blustery men who were always in a hurry. They would call out their orders in a very loud voice, right over Ronnie's head, and the grocery man wouldn't even notice that Ronnie was already saying, "Please, sir—"

"I guess only big people count," thought Ronnie. "I wish I were big."

6

He wished it again when his mother took him to the great store downtown.

"I can ride on the escalator, Mommie," he said happily, "while you go and buy your things."

"I'm sorry, honey," his mother said. "The sign says no children can go on it without a big person."

"Oh, I do wish I were big," said Ronnie.

Then one day something happened! He went with his mother to the zoo. Ronnie liked animals. "I would like to have one to play with at home," he said. A giraffe looked over the wall just as if he heard.

"Not you," laughed Ronnie. "You're too tall!"

He laughed again to think of taking home a giraffe.

8

He watched boys put peanuts in the end of the elephant's long trunk. "I could use an elephant," he said. "If I dropped something out of the window, he could pick it up with his trunk."

"But he'd crowd us terribly," his mother replied, and they laughed, thinking of an elephant in their home.

9

The seals lived in a big pool. They were very noisy. They
flopped in and out of the water and made great splashes.
They barked and barked like dogs.

"I shouldn't like a seal for a pet," Ronnie decided. "He'd
be too spattery. He'd fill up our whole bathtub. Then how
could we take any baths?"

10

Ronnie's mother had to go to telephone his daddy. It was too long a walk for Ronnie, so she said, "You could wait here by the Children's Zoo until I come back. I won't be long, and I'll ask this man at the gate to take care of you."

So Ronnie sat down on the grass near the gate.

11

He could see the tops of small buildings beyond the gate
and hear the noises of little animals. He could see children
riding on ponies. How Ronnie would have liked to ride a
pony! But you had to buy a ticket to go inside, and Ronnie
had no money.

"Only big people have money," thought Ronnie. "I wish
I were big." It was then that THE THING happened.

A man carrying a box had been walking back and forth. He kept looking through the gate of the Children's Zoo as if he wanted to go in. Every little while he would look at Ronnie, as if he knew him.

Now he stopped in front of Ronnie and lifted his hat.

"Excuse me, sir," said the man. "My name is Johnson. I live next door to you. Could I ask a favor of you?"

Ronnie smiled and said, "Yes, I know you." He wondered what was in Mr. Johnson's box. He wondered what he could do for a big man like Mr. Johnson.

"I happen to have two tickets to the Children's Zoo," said Mr. Johnson, "but I am not allowed inside unless I am accompanied by a child." He pointed to a sign and read:

CHILDREN'S ZOO

NO GROWNUP ADMITTED UNACCOMPANIED

BY A CHILD

"I do want to go in," said Mr. Johnson, looking sad.

Ronnie knew just how he felt. He jumped up.

"I will help you," he said, putting his hand into Mr. Johnson's empty one. Then he asked the man at the gate, "May I take Mr. Johnson inside? He lives next door to us, and he has tickets."

The man at the gate smiled. "Sure," he answered, "since he's a friend of yours. I'll tell your mother where you are." And he opened the gate.

Ronnie and Mr. Johnson went through the gate.

"This is most kind of you," said Mr. Johnson.

First they came to a little cavelike house with LOW BRIDGE
over the door. The door was just the right size for Ronnie,
and he was sorry for Mr. Johnson.

"You'll have to bend way down," he warned, "or you'll
bump your head. There are some goldfish inside."

"Thank you for telling me," said Mr. Johnson, stooping
down.

16

A bigger house was called the Noah's Ark. Mr. Johnson read a sign on it—NO ADULTS ALLOWED. He said sadly, "I'm afraid that means me. Perhaps you'll go in and tell me what is there?" Ronnie was glad to.

"They're rabbits!" he reported, and Mr. Johnson declared, "I don't know what I should have done without you."

Honk and Tonk were two big geese that were in a kind of summer house. Ronnie patted one, but he didn't know whether it was Honk or Tonk.

So he patted the other one, too.

18

When the geese were thirsty, a keeper took them over to
a little pool with a fountain.

"That is very kind of the keeper," said Ronnie.

"It is indeed," said Mr. Johnson.

In a fenced-in place were a mother goat and a kid.

"I never saw a baby goat before," said Ronnie. "I like the little animals best."

"I, too," said Mr. Johnson.

20

They passed a spotted fawn, and Mr. Johnson said, "It is a baby deer. I think he is even prettier than a big deer."

"I, too," said Ronnie.

21

A loud "Ba-a" made Ronnie turn around.
"A black sheep!" Mr. Johnson exclaimed.

> *Baa, baa, black sheep,*
> *Have you any wool?*

Ronnie, who knew that poem, answered,

> *Yes, sir, yes, sir,*
> *Three bags full!*

Then they laughed and together they went on,

> *One for my master,*
> *One for my dame,*
> *And one for the little boy*
> *Who lives in the lane.*

"It's nice we both think of the same things," said Ronnie.
"It is indeed," agreed Mr. Johnson.

22

They passed some Bantam chicks that were all soft and fluffy. The chicks kept crying, "Peep! Peep!" while the mother hen scratched the ground.

"I guess they're hungry," said Ronnie.

"There's no doubt of it," answered Mr. Johnson.

24

Some puppies nearby were barking, "Yap! Yap!"

"I think they want to play with us," said Ronnie.

"I'm sure of it," said Mr. Johnson, stopping to play. The puppies rolled over and pretended to bite. They tried to get hold of Mr. Johnson's box.

*W*hen Ronnie stood up again, he saw two little boys riding ponies. Mr. Johnson saw them, too.

Mr. Johnson sighed. "I always wanted to ride a pony," he said. "But I'm too big. I shall never know how it feels—unless" —he stopped and looked at Ronnie—"unless you would do me the very great favor of taking a ride for me so you could tell me?"

"Oh, yes," Ronnie answered quickly. "I'd like to."

It was no time at all before he was on a pony's back.

"It's fun!" he shouted as the pony started off. Mr. Johnson tipped his hat.

When Ronnie came back, he told his friend all about it. "It was nice when the pony just walked. I felt up high. When he trotted fast, it jiggled me, but it was a nice feeling. It's too bad," he said, looking at Mr. Johnson, "that you're so big."

"It is indeed," said Mr. Johnson, "but I do thank you for being small enough to ride for me."

"You're welcome," replied Ronnie.

27

"Now let us visit the Wishing Seat," suggested Mr. Johnson.

"What is a Wishing Seat?" asked Ronnie.

"Well, it's a big flat stone where children sit and make a wish, the way I wished for you to bring me in here."

"Oh," said Ronnie and sat down on the stone.

He remembered the wish he was always wishing. "I wish
I weren't so little."

He *almost said it*, but stopped himself. If he had been big,
he never could have given Mr. Johnson such a happy day.
He jumped up.

"I don't want to make a wish!" he shouted. His mother
who was outside the gate heard him.

"There's my honey!" she cried.

"Mommie!" he called back and ran to her. "Mommie, I went to the Children's Zoo. I liked the little animals best. I helped Mr. Johnson. He couldn't go in without me. And I rode on a pony for him because he was too big. He said I was very kind. It's a good thing I'm little, isn't it?"

30

Mr. Johnson handed Ronnie the box he carried.

"Madame," he said to Ronnie's mother, "I have been looking for a small, kind child like your son, who likes little animals. The box is for him. Good day."

He tipped his hat and left, while Ronnie's mother was saying, "Thank you, Mr. Johnson!" and Ronnie was squealing, "It's a little turtle, Mommie, a dear little turtle!"

32

Ronnie's Wish

RONNIE lives in a great big city where there are busy streets, subways, escalators, and crowds of people. Ronnie often feels very small in the big city, with all the many people who are bigger than he is.

Ronnie does not have lots of animals to play with, as country children do. He does not have little pigs and calves and lambs for pets. When he wants to see a lot of animals, he has to go to the zoo. All sorts of animals, like giraffes and elephants and seals, are kept in the zoo. One day Ronnie goes to see them, and he makes a big discovery. That's what this story is about.

The author, Jeanette Perkins Brown, has written stories for children and told many, many more. She knows the kind of stories that children like.

Other books in the Little Playmate Series are *Keiko's Birthday*, which tells what happened at school when Keiko was five, and *Nezbah's Lamb*, which is about a little girl and her lamb who live in the Navaho country.

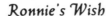
4908